CHAMPIONS
ON THE
BENCH

The Cannon Street YMCA All-Stars

by **Carole Boston Weatherford**

illustrations by **Leonard Jenkins**

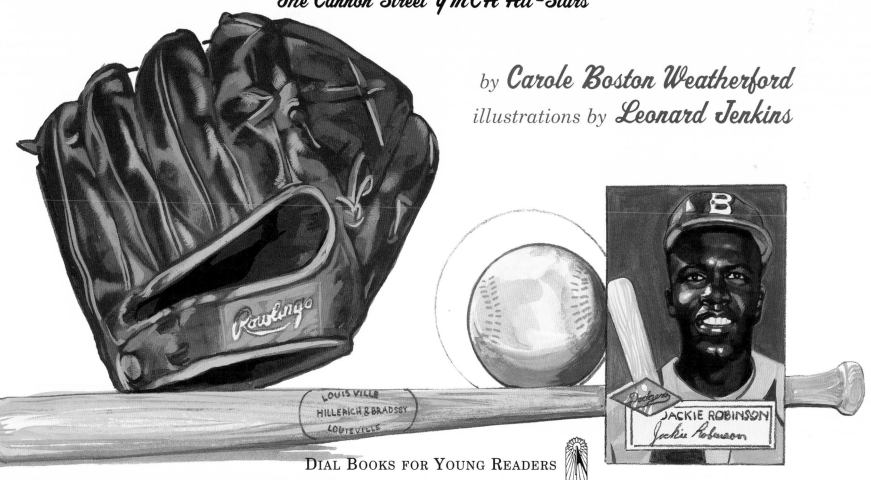

Rawlings

LOUISVILLE
HILLERICH & BRADSBY
LOUISVILLE

JACKIE ROBINSON
Jackie Robinson

DIAL BOOKS FOR YOUNG READERS

ROY CAMPANELLA

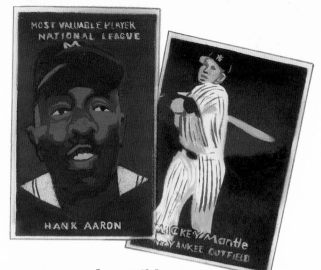

MOST VALUABLE PLAYER NATIONAL LEAGUE

HANK AARON

MICKEY Mantle
N.Y. YANKEE OUTFIELD

Summer was finally here and all my baseball dreams seemed possible.

Willie Mays was leading the major league in home runs. Hank Aaron made the all-star team. Roy Campanella was on his way to becoming the National League's Most Valuable Player.

And I had just joined the Cannon Street YMCA Little League— the only colored Little League in all of South Carolina. Daddy signed me up for the Police Athletic League team the very first day.

We sure looked like winners in our brand-new uniforms. Soon as we got them, we posed for team pictures. "Say, 'Play ball!'" the photographer said.

We learned to pitch, hit, and catch. I practiced stealing bases. "Slide, Cleveland!" Coach shouted.

When I got home, Mama would say, "These pants look like you play on your knees."

And as soon as he came in from work, Daddy helped me with my swing.

Coach Gibson tried every player on the bases and in the outfield. Then he assigned our positions. "Congratulations, Cleveland. You're our pitcher," he said, patting my back.

"I won't let you down," I told Coach.

Our first game at Harmon Field was against the Pan-Hellenic team. I was kind of nervous, but I pitched like I'd been doing it forever. I only gave up five hits. Plus I hit a double that drove in a run. We won 4–0.

Tasty Cone Ice Cream Shoppe

Fi
Ho

Week after week on the dusty field in sweltering heat, we played to win.
Some of the boys on the Pan-Hellenic, Fielding Home for Funerals, and
Harleston Funeral teams, I knew from school, church, or the neighborhood.
We all wanted the same thing—to become all-stars.

At the end of the season, Coach picked the all-stars. Only all-stars got to play in the state tournament. And if we won there, we'd go to the World Series play-offs. My name was the last one he called.

That night, I slept with my baseball cap on and dreamed that the Cannon Street All-Stars had won the state tournament. My teammates were lifting me on their shoulders as my whole family waved from the stands. The dream seemed so real and I woke up sure we could make it to the World Series.

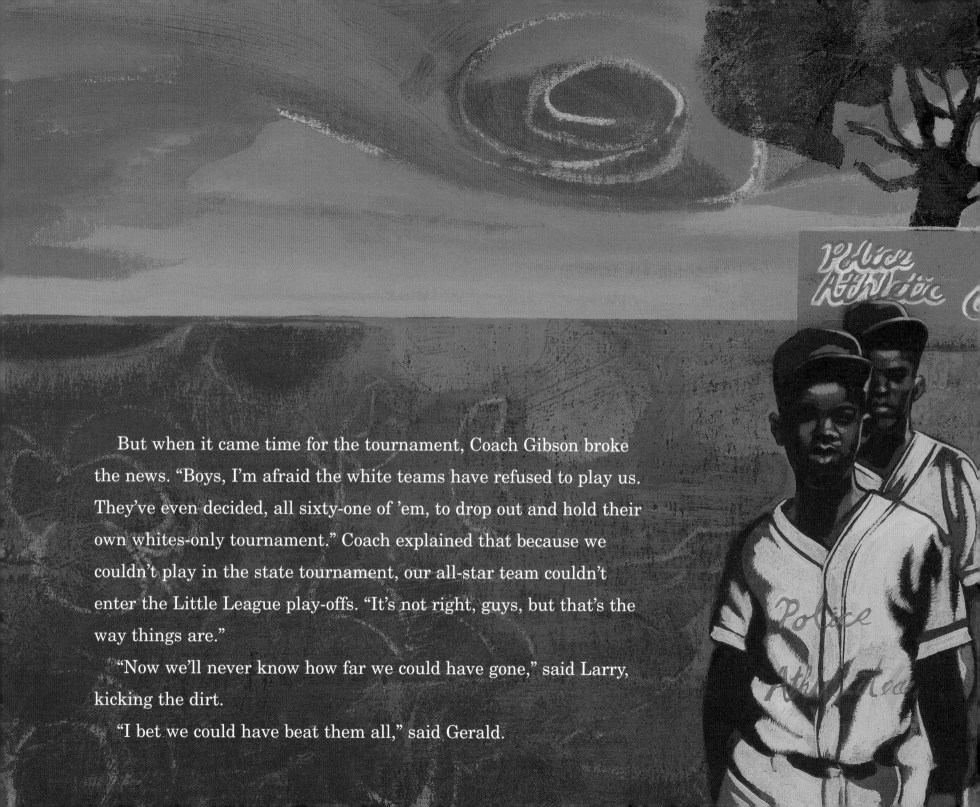

But when it came time for the tournament, Coach Gibson broke the news. "Boys, I'm afraid the white teams have refused to play us. They've even decided, all sixty-one of 'em, to drop out and hold their own whites-only tournament." Coach explained that because we couldn't play in the state tournament, our all-star team couldn't enter the Little League play-offs. "It's not right, guys, but that's the way things are."

"Now we'll never know how far we could have gone," said Larry, kicking the dirt.

"I bet we could have beat them all," said Gerald.

We knew we were as good as any team. Sometimes we played with boys from the white leagues in sandlot games. Leon, the best batter in our league, had racked up a string of homers, and Gerald stole bases faster than the blink of an eye.

"Y'all are good," said Tommy, a pitcher from a white team. "Too bad the tournament is off."

"Yeah," said Leon. "We would have whipped your team."

"Maybe," said Tommy, "but I wouldn't be so sure."

I was surprised when the national Little League invited us to its World Series. They said we would be their guests. A yellow school bus took us all the way from Charleston to Williamsport, Pennsylvania. I had never been so far from home.

In Pennsylvania, I met boys from all over the country. We bunked in a college dormitory, ate side by side, and traded baseball cards right and left. "I'll trade you Mickey Mantle for Hank Aaron," said a boy from Ohio.

"No way!" I told him.

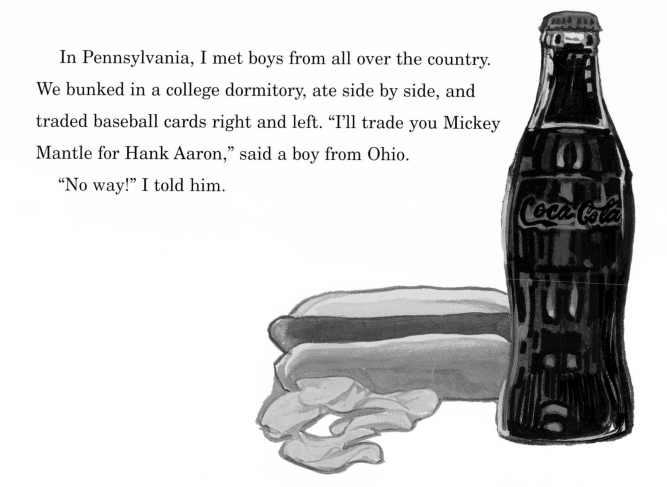

While all the other teams played, we had to watch from the stands. Some of the players were almost as good as the pros. "I can't believe we came this far just to sit," I grumbled.

"Me neither," huffed James.

"It ain't fair," said Russell, shaking his head.

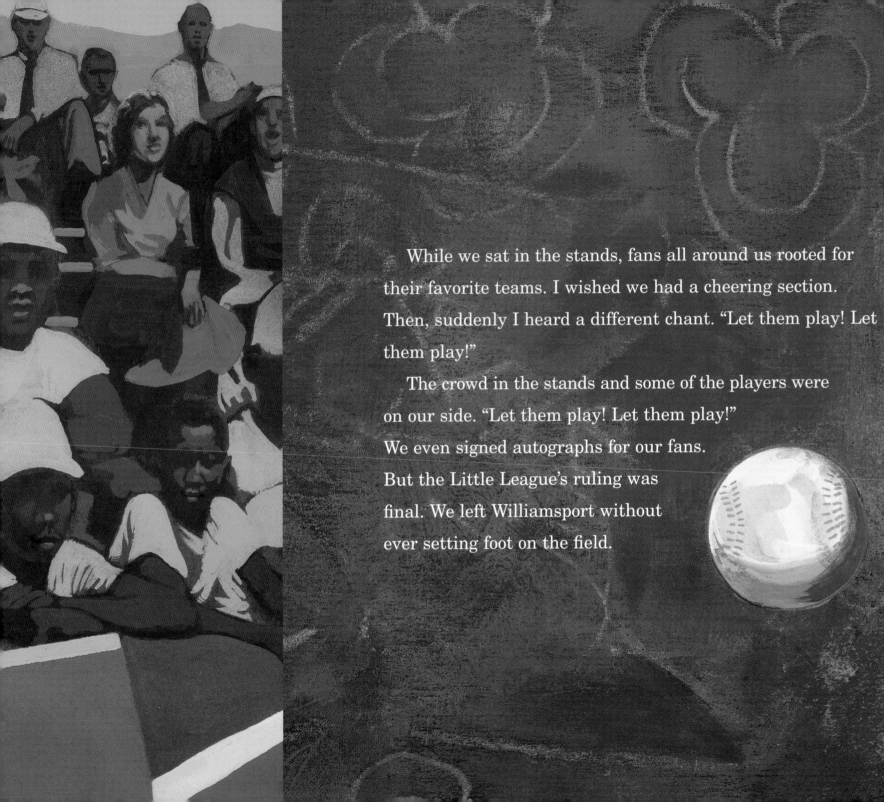

While we sat in the stands, fans all around us rooted for their favorite teams. I wished we had a cheering section. Then, suddenly I heard a different chant. "Let them play! Let them play!"

The crowd in the stands and some of the players were on our side. "Let them play! Let them play!" We even signed autographs for our fans. But the Little League's ruling was final. We left Williamsport without ever setting foot on the field.

"There'll be other seasons," said Coach as we boarded the bus for the ride south. I pulled my cap down over my eyes to hide how cheated I felt. Coach sat beside me. "You all right, Cleveland?"

"I'm never going to play ball again," I swore.

"Then the teams who wouldn't play you will have won," said Coach. "You have to keep playing, so you'll be ready when you finally face the white teams. They can't avoid you forever."

"I'll show them," I said.

"I bet you will," said Coach.

Back home, wherever I went, grown-ups stopped me and said, "Y'all really made us proud."

Summer was winding down and our Little League season was over. But even without coaches or crowds or uniforms, we played ball every day after school.

At the end of September, though, we dropped our bats and gathered around the TV set. The Brooklyn Dodgers and the New York Yankees were battling it out in the World Series. Daddy and I didn't miss one play. He'd been a Dodgers fan ever since they signed

Jackie Robinson. I saw black players on other teams now, but Daddy always reminded me that Jackie was the first. Jackie was his hero. Daddy is mine.

Daddy and I both leaped to our feet when Jackie Robinson stole home in the eighth inning of game one. "I've never seen a play like that!" I yelled.

All through the series, Daddy prodded the players as if they could hear him through the TV set. "Got to do better than that!" he fussed when Don Newcombe gave up two home runs to the Yankees.

And even though we were rooting for the Dodgers, I clapped when Elston Howard, the first black Yankee, homered. "Not bad for a rookie," said Daddy.

Daddy fretted when Jackie got hurt and the series was tied 3–3. We could see Jackie was still rallying his teammates from the sidelines during the final game.

With a score of 2–0, Jackie Robinson and the Brooklyn Dodgers won their first World Series championship! And, somehow, I felt like we had *all* won.

1955

The 1955 Cannon Street team watch the Little League World Series from the stands

This story is inspired by the real-life 1955 Cannon Street YMCA Little League All-Stars. In 1955, the Cannon Street YMCA in Charleston chartered a Little League. With four teams—the Fielding Home for Funerals, Harleston Funeral Home, Pan-Hellenic, and Police Athletic League—it was the only Little League in South Carolina for African Americans. The other sixty-one chartered Little League programs in the state were composed entirely of white people. Until then, no South Carolina teams with African American players had entered the postseason tournament to vie for a bid at the Little League Baseball World Series.

In the summer of 1955, all sixty-one white leagues refused to play the Cannon Street YMCA All-Stars. As a result, the Little League barred the white leagues from the tournament. The white leagues formed their own program, Dixie Baseball for Boys, and held their own tournament.

The Cannon Street YMCA All-Stars were crowned state champions, but—according to Little League rules—could not advance to the play-offs because the team had won the tournament by forfeit rather than on-the-field play. However, the Little League invited the team to be its guests at the World Series in Williamsport, Pennsylvania. The fourteen boys on the Cannon Street YMCA All-Stars sat in the stands and never got to play one game. "We could have won the whole thing," Vermont Brown, one of the team's power hitters, said forty-seven years later. "We were that good."

In 1955 some northern and western Little Leagues were already integrated. Nevertheless, white leagues in the South thought Little League should not meddle in what they considered local matters. Hundreds of southern white leagues left the Little League program in protest. After the civil rights movement, race relations improved. African American teams not only played white teams, African Americans and whites became teammates.

In 2002, the Cannon Street YMCA All-Stars returned to Williamsport. They lined up on the field during opening ceremonies of the Little League Baseball World Series. "There is no way to right the wrong perpetrated on the boys of the Cannon Street YMCA Little League team . . . because of their skin color," Stephen D. Keener, president of Little League Baseball, said. "Little League will be honored to have the Cannon Street team with us as our special guests."

The team players were: John Bailey, Charles Bradley, Vermont Brown, William Godfrey, Vernon C. Grey, Allen Jackson, Carl Johnson, John Mack, Leroy Major, David Middleton, Arthur Peoples, John Rivers, Norman Robinson, and Maurice Singleton. Alternates are Leroy Carter and George Gregory. Coaches and founders were Lee J. Bennett, Walter Burke, Rufus Dilligard, A. O. Graham, Robert Morrison, R. H. Penn, and Benjamin Singleton.

The team's star pitchers were Allen Jackson and Leroy Major. The strongest hitters were Vermont Brown, Allen Jackson, and Buck Godfrey, who went on to become a championship high school football coach.

Today, a plaque at Charleston's ballpark honors the Cannon Street YMCA Little League All-Stars.

Members of the Cannon Street team of 1955 are honored at the 2002 Little League World Series

For Mommy and Ron, who champion all my pursuits.
In memory of my all-star, "Bus" —you still shine in my heart.
—C.B.W.

For Yaway
—L.J.

DIAL BOOKS FOR YOUNG READERS
A division of Penguin Young Readers Group
Published by The Penguin Group
Penguin Group (USA) Inc., 375 Hudson Street, New York, NY 10014, U.S.A.
Penguin Group (Canada), 90 Eglinton Avenue East, Suite 700, Toronto, Ontario, Canada M4P 2Y3
(a division of Pearson Penguin Canada Inc.)
Penguin Books Ltd, 80 Strand, London WC2R 0RL, England
Penguin Ireland, 25 St. Stephen's Green, Dublin 2, Ireland (a division of Penguin Books Ltd)
Penguin Books India Pvt Ltd, 11 Community Centre, Panchsheel Park, New Delhi - 110 017, India
Penguin Group (NZ), Cnr Airborne and Rosedale Roads, Albany, Auckland, New Zealand
(a division of Pearson New Zealand Ltd)
Penguin Books (South Africa) (Pty) Ltd, 24 Sturdee Avenue, Rosebank, Johannesburg 2196, South Africa
Penguin Books Ltd, Registered Offices: 80 Strand, London WC2R 0RL, England

Text copyright © 2007 by Carole Boston Weatherford
Illustrations copyright © 2007 by Leonard Jenkins
Photographs courtesy of Little League Baseball and Softball
All rights reserved
The publisher does not have any control over
and does not assume any responsibility for author or
third-party websites or their content.
Designed by Jasmin Rubero
Text set in New Century School Book
Manufactured in China on acid-free paper

1 3 5 7 9 10 8 6 4 2

Library of Congress Cataloging-in-Publication Data
Weatherford, Carole Boston, date.
Champions on the bench : the Cannon Street YMCA All-Stars /
by Carole Boston Weatherford ; illustrations by Leonard Jenkins.
p   cm.
Summary: Story based on the discrimination faced by the 1955 Cannon
Street YMCA Little League All-Stars when the white teams refused to play them in the series tournament.
ISBN 978-0-8037-2987-2
[1. Baseball—Fiction. 2. Little League baseball—Fiction. 3. Race discrimination—Fiction.
4. African Americans—Fiction. 5. South Carolina—Fiction.] I. Jenkins, Leonard, ill. II. Title.
PZ7.W3535Le 2007
[Fic]—dc22   2003019385

Paintings were created with pencil, acrylic, and spray paint on illustration board.